JUV/E   Ichikawa, Satomi.
FIC
          Nora's surprise.

$14.95

DATE			
10-94			

BAKER & TAYLOR

To Mr. and Mrs. H. Imamura,
with my warmest good wishes

Nora's Surprise

SATOMI ICHIKAWA

PHILOMEL BOOKS

One summer day, a letter arrived at Nora's house. On it, in big letters, was written the word "INVITATION."

Nora called her three friends, Maggie the doll, Teddy the bear, and Kiki the dog. Then, in a loud voice, she read the invitation to them:

"Please come to our tea party. There'll be lots to eat.

We have a big garden to play in, and a swimming pool too. Signed,

The geese in the wood on the edge of the village."

A big garden with a swimming pool! And lots to eat!
Nora and her friends picked a large bunch of flowers to
take as a present and immediately set off.

"Hello! So glad you could come!" said the geese, who met their guests at the door.

"Oh my!" said Nora. She had expected a different sort of house.

She turned to see a great woolly sheep with his head in the flowers she had brought! "Who is that?" Nora asked.

"Benjy, from next door," said one goose. "You're just in time, Benjy. Come and join us."

But Benjy was just too big. He got stuck. And
they couldn't get him through the door.

"All right, then," said the geese. "Let's take everything
into the garden. We'll have a picnic instead."

What treats there were!

Carrot juice, buckwheat bread and cakes, raspberry jam, cucumber sandwiches, and spinach biscuits.

Soon the table was full of food, and sitting right in the middle were Nora's flowers. They looked lovely.

But no sooner had everyone sat down than Benjy stuck his head into the cucumber sandwiches and began eating them up.

After that he finished the raspberry jam and...

"Grab something, before everything disappears!"
said Maggie the doll, and she reached for the cookies.

The picnic had turned into a free-for-all.